Triska

by Morton Otwell Gourdneck

To Shana. You finally got your adventure. I'm sorry it took so long.

Dear reader,

as you journey into this book, you will learn of a young lady that stumbles upon a forgotten mystery from long ago. As she searches for answers in the small community of Pulltight, it seems the past begins to answer her call. Could it be that after a season in Hell, the undead have returned to ask for help? Or worse yet, to feed?

If you scare easy, my proofreader has asked that you please do not read this book. It should be placed far away, high on a shelf, out of your reach. She has also asked that I never write a book such as this again, as it caused her much fear and distress. I did however calm her nerves, assuring her that only a small percentage of the book was actual truth. Especially the part about vampires.

If you do decide to go through with reading the book, I hope that you will enjoy it and also keep some garlic or perhaps holy water close to your side. Vampires like to watch from unseen places as you read about them.

Happy reading and my greatest wish is that someday, when the time comes, you die only from natural causes.

Sincerely,

M.O.G.

Chapter 1
Pulltight!

"Do you remember the story I told you about how 'Pulltight' got its name?" Grandpa Bill Dotson asked his granddaughter, Shana, as they turned down the small gravel road that led to his house.

"How could I forget, Grandpa, you tell me every summer," Shana said with a chuckle. "Refresh my memory, just in case I forgot something."

Grandpa Bill smiled at his pretty, brown haired granddaughter that seemed to have grown up right before his very eyes. Although he would never say, he was a proud man at the moment to have Shana back with him.

"Well, you see, there used to be a school house here in the community back in the early 20s. Lots of farm kids lived in the area and most were as tough as all get out. It wasn't uncommon for a fight to break out on the way to school in the mornings, mostly boys, but sometimes even the girls would take to scrapping. One morning a group of kids were on their way to class and two of the young ladies went to exchanging words and one thing led to another. They threw their books on the ground and a crowd started gathering around them in a big circle. A few licks were thrown by each girl, but they soon grabbed a hold of one another's hair and locked on. They were slinging each other all over the place by their hair and all of the kids went to hollering 'Pull tight! Pull tight!' A couple of farmers came and broke the fight up. They sent the kids on to school, but couldn't stop laughing about what they had just witnessed. A couple of years later, one of those farmers ran for County Judge and recalled the incident when the State of Arkansas recommended they name the community. He just laughed and said, 'The name of that little place is Pulltight, Arkansas.' And that's how we got our name."

Shana smiled and rolled her eyes. It was a corny, hick story but she loved the way Grandpa Bill told it. It was something she looked forward to each summer when she came to stay with him. Pulltight was a long way from her home in Galesburg, Illinois, but she enjoyed the country life.

Although there was the same familiar spark of excitement from being back, a certain sadness tried to take its place. This was the summer that Shana had turned eighteen and she couldn't help but wonder if this might be her last summer at Grandpa Bill's. College would be coming up soon and she would be away for the next four years.

Walking into the old wooden house was like a trip back in time. Everything seemed so strikingly picturesque. The old cast iron skillets hung on the walls, one sitting on the cook stove, half filled with homemade biscuits. Jars of canned vegetables lined the shelves and rooster décor seemed to fill every empty space on the walls. Shana began to chuckle as she spotted a wooden shelf on the wall. "Got any new land, Grandpa Bill?" She asked.

"Ah, one or two new pieces," he said, walking over and taking a jar from the shelf.

Grandpa Bill had been collecting land for many years now. There were several pint jars of dirt, lining the shelves. Each with a name taped to the side. It was his goal in life to own a piece of land from every wealthy property owner in the county. Every now and then, he'd make a trip to one of their properties and take a scoop of dirt, putting it in a jar. He claimed that this made him one of the wealthiest land owners in the area.

"I recently came into some Abernathy land," he said with a smile. "You know, they just put five natural gas wells on that property this year."

Shana just smiled and shook her head. She knew this must be where she got her unique style of thinking. It had to be inherited, because no one else in their right mind would come up with those kinds of thoughts.

“You go ahead and get settled,” Grandpa Bill said. “I know you’ve got a lot of unpacking to do. If things all fall into place, we may take a trip into town tomorrow morning. I need to pick up a few things at the store. I sure miss the old days when Pulltight had its own little store. Not much need for one now, I reckon. These days its just me and that Darby bunch down the road. This old town is just fading away.”

“Pulltight is still rich in history, Grandpa Bill. I can’t wait to get out there in the woods and start digging through the old bottle dump again. Last year, I found so many good ones. I even found a few from the late 1800s. I had one for everything you could thing of, having the mange, the chills and the grip.”

“Well, if you find any more of those, bring me a couple, I’ve had every one of those things this year and I need a cure.”

Shana laughed out loud as she started towards her bedroom. “I’ll do that, Grandpa Bill, we can’t have you down with the mange, now, can we?”

Chapter 2
The Dig

The garden hoe clicked the edge of the glass bottles as Shana sifted through the leaves and dirt. Soon she spotted a blue bottle and carefully dug around the edges, trying hard not to break it. She hoped it would be a whole one with no busted pieces or nicks. She smiled when she realized it was complete.

"Another for the sack," she said, carefully placing it into a brown paper bag she brought with her.

There was nothing she enjoyed more than walking through the woods or the creeks, searching for things from the past. With each relic, she would try to imagine the person who last used it, how they must have been and the quality of life they lived.

As the garden hoe continued to scrape against the old bottles another sound echoed in the distance - thunder. Shana cringed as she looked at the sky. It was almost black now and she could see the rain falling through the clouds in the distance. She knew there would be no way to make it back to Grandpa Bill's house in time to beat it. Her adventurous spirit had led her too deeply into the woods. She knew of only one other place close by that might offer some sort of temporary shelter - Fletcher Cemetery. It was a very old cemetery with stones dating back as early at the 1820's. She had gone there from time to time to read the engravings. A single mausoleum sat atop a hill in the cemetery and this was the only thought of refuge that came to mind.

Shana ran quickly along a slough in the woods until she could see the white and granite headstones sticking up in the distance. There among them was an ancient, red bricked mausoleum. She looked back at the clouds once more. Although hesitant, she knew she must stick to her original plan. When she reached the mausoleum, the old iron door was half open. It creaked and echoed off thc bricks. She stepped sheepishly inside, squatting down in the corner, just beside the two concrete tombs that inhabited it. She had made it just in time. The rain began to beat heavily on the roof, some splashing in through one of the broken windows.

In times past, Shana had never been afraid to be in the cemetery, it seemed like such a peaceful place. This time, however, there seemed to be a darkness that loomed with the storm. The wind raged as the lighting flashed and all became cold within the brick structure. Shana began to tremble and her thoughts soon turned to many "What if's."

This was one of the most violent storms she had ever encountered. She was sure that she heard a tree uprooting in the distance and she began to cry. Through her tears, Shana could hear the storm coming to a halt. She sat very still and waited just a bit, making sure it would be clear outside. All was quiet, completely quiet. She jumped as she heard an eerie whisper coming from just outside the mausoleum. "Triska. Triska," it said.

Shana stood up and walked to the door, looking outside. She had been correct, a huge walnut tree had uprooted just along the cemetery's edge. "Who's out here?" She asked. "Is there someone who got trapped in the storm? Do you need my help?"

No one seemed to be outside so Shana made her way out onto the wet grass. The raindrops bled through her shoes as she walked along. A quick breeze suddenly blew over her skin, giving her an icy chill. "Triska. Triska," said a voice, from the nearby trees. Fear set in and Shana got the feeling that she was no longer alone. She slowly walked back into the woods and along the slough where she had been hunting bottles. The brown paper bag she had filled with relics was now soaking wet and falling apart. As she reached down to pick it up, there was a sound of bushes moving in the distance. Her eyes fell on them and she was sure she could make out the figure of a girl standing behind them. "Triska," the figure whispered.

Shana walked slowly towards the bushes, holding her breath as she tried to summon courage with each new step. Reaching the bushes, she slowly put in her hands, pulling them back to reveal the person on the other side. To her surprise, there was no one there. She was sure that a girl had been standing there just seconds before. She searched the ground for footprints in the fresh, wet dirt but found none. But what she did see, shining on the ground, was a dull, yellow ring with a green stone. Shana grabbed it up and examined it. It appeared to be a ladies 10K gold promise ring. She quickly placed it on her finger, turned and ran back to Grandpa Bill's house. She knew he must be worried, and she also knew that something very unusual had just taken place. She would need some time to sort this out. Whose ring could this be? And, what did "Triska" mean?

Chapter 3
Darby Knows Best

Daggett was just like any other southern, hole in the wall, small town. Not much to look at, but compared to the community of Pulltight, it was a big city. Grandpa Bill traveled to Daggett from time to time and spent most of the day and evening there. He claimed he was going there for groceries and supplies, but really, he spent his time hanging around the parts store just shooting the breeze with the other old men in town. He never went through the front entrance, always through the back door. Shana would tease him and say it was the "V.I.P. entrance." He would always smile that big proud smile of his, straighten his hat and throw the screen door open. Moments later, you could hear the men inside kidding him and he would start in with the witty comebacks. This always signaled it was her time to make the rounds in town. Most stops included the Five and Dime, Jackson's Book Store and of course the Majestic Theatre.

As Shana entered the theatre, she studied the red carpet and the flashing movie poster sign. The smell of fresh popcorn was around every corner and she could almost taste the salt and butter as she took a deep whiff. Over by the concession stand stood six of the Darby kids. They were from Pulltight as well. Most of them were known for being a little on the wild side, even the smallest ones. Shana recalled the summer they all got head lice. Their daddy shaved every one of their heads, even the girls. It was a sad sight to her, those young girls walking around in dresses and bald heads. "Some people are just down right ignorant," she thought. "Why would a parent do that to their children. A good washing with tea tree oil would have done just fine."

Shana's attention focused back on the concession stand. She couldn't see what was going on, but some sort of excitement was taking place. The Darby's were gathered all around and sticking their fingers out towards something.

From around the corner, a hunched over old man, wearing his red theatre uniform, scooted in the Darbys' direction. "Please, please don't do that," he said. "Please, just stand back, children. I wouldn't want it to bite you."

All the Darbys backed away and Shana moved in a little closer. There, sitting on the corner of the snack bar, just next to the popcorn machine, was a large fluffy rat. "Sir," One of the Darby kids asked. "why do you have a pet rat in the snack bar? Isn't that bad for business?"

"We don't have a pet rat," The old man replied. "This is the first time I've ever seen it."

"Sir, that rat's starting to wobble around. I think he's going to die," A Darby girl said, pointing to the counter.

The old man smiled at the children and in his most polite voice replied, "Yes, we put something out for him earlier this morning."

Suddenly, the rat fell off the counter and began kicking on the floor. The old man took his time retrieving a popcorn box. He soon came back around the corner, grabbed the kicking rat by the tail and placed it in the box. "I'll take the poor little fellow outside," he said with a smile.

Everyone stood staring in disbelief of what had happened, especially Shana. It was the first time she had ever really seen a rat up close.

"You kids want some popcorn or not," the Concession lady asked in a rude voice. "I don't have all afternoon."

All the Darby's looked at one another and said, "No!" in unison.

"Oh, come on, kids," Dale Darby, the oldest of the bunch said. "Have some popcorn. It's special popcorn. It has raisins in it."

"EWWW," shouted the younger kids, running from the concession stand and into the theatre to find their seats.

"Hey, don't be a wise guy," the concession lady shouted. "I have to sell this stuff! You Darby's are bad for business!"

"Um, no ma'am, I think your rats are bad for business," Dale replied. "You should really have a talk with them."

This brought a laugh from Shana, which caught the attention of Dale.

"Hey, Miss Dotson, right? You're that Yankee girl from up around Illinois. You sure grew up," a lanky, redheaded Dale Darby said, walking up to her, with a mischievous smile on his face.

"Yankee?" She asked. "You say that like it's a bad thing. And what do you mean by 'you sure grew up?' You're the same age as me, Dale Darby."

"I guess you're right. I just didn't know if you remembered me or not."

"Oh, I remember you. You've never really said much to me, but I used to watch you and your brothers and sisters play freeze tag in your yard when I went walking down Grandpa Bill's road. I remember one time, you knocked the sheets off your momma's clothes line and I saw you get a whipping. Your momma grabbed a piece of a toy racecar track off the porch and wore you out with it. Do you remember that?"

Dale's face turned a bright red. He was usually pretty quick with the comebacks but Shana had him at a loss for words. "You saw that did you?"

"Oh yeah, I won't ever forget that."

"I won't either. I still have the lines from that race track imprinted on the back of my legs. Momma don't play around when she gets mad. She grabs whatever's handy and goes to whipping."

"I'll bet you do remember," Shana said with a wicked smile. "Hey, Dale, since we're neighbors and all, I wanted to ask you a question. You know Pulltight pretty well, right? I mean, the history and such of the town?"

"Well, I have been there my whole life and I guess my family has been, too. Probably since the beginning. What is it you're getting at?"

"Sometimes I find things, you know, bottles, old coins and stuff out in the woods or creeks. I was just wondering if I showed you some things, you might know who they belonged to?"

"They could belong to anybody, I guess," Dale replied. "I find marbles in the fields all the time. There's no way of knowing who they belong to. I just put them in a jar and keep them on my nightstand. It would be impossible to pinpoint the owner. Unless… Unless I found a really special one. Say, you didn't find something special, did you?"

Shana looked around the theatre lobby to make sure no one were listening in. The only one around was the old man who had just taken the rat outside. He didn't seem like much of a concern but still she leaned in and whispered, "I think maybe I did." Holding out her hand, she showed Dale the golden promise ring with the green stone.

"Oh, wow. That's a Jim Dandy of a ring, ain't it? You find that in the creek?"

"No, I really don't want to say, not just now. And there's a little more to the story. Do you think you could help me?"

Dale studied the ring a bit more and gave her a look of confidence. "I can do that," he said.

"Will you meet me tomorrow?" Shana asked.

"Yeah, when I finish my chores. Where do you want to meet?"

“Fletcher’s Cemetery. At the old mausoleum.”

“Whew, that’s a heck of a meeting place,” Dale said, pushing his hair back with his hand. “Why there?”

“I’ll explain when you get there. Will you meet me? Two o’ clock?”

“I’ll do it.”

“Good, I’ll see you there,” Shana said with a smile.

“Say, you wanna sit with me during the movie,” Dale asked.

“Are you sitting with your brothers and sisters?”

“Yeah, I have to. I gotta keep an eye on them.”

“No thanks,” Shana replied. “No offence but I’m not going anywhere near that rowdy bunch. I’ll take my chances with the rats.”

“I don’t blame you,” Dale replied. “If they weren’t related to me, I wouldn’t sit with them either.

Shana chuckled as she and Dale both headed in to see the movie.

Chapter 4
Do you know who?

Shana waited patiently at the edge of Fletcher's cemetery. She stood close by the walnut tree that had uprooted during the storm, peeking around it, watching for any unusual movements. Within minutes, she saw what appeared to be a tall shadow making its way along the opposite side. Stooping down, she soon recognized the familiar sound of whistling. It was Dale Darby and he appeared to be looking over his shoulder.

"Not afraid, are you?" Shana said, jumping from behind the tree and giving him a start.

"Not at all," Dale replied smoothly. "I always whistle when I walk. It lets the bears know I'm coming and gives them a chance to run and hide from me."

"Yeah, right. Well, anyway, you're probably wondering why I wanted to meet you here. I've been thinking it over and I'm not so sure I want to tell you anymore. I think I've changed my mind."

"Oh no," Dale said, holding a hand up to Shana's face. "You've got me curious, there's no going back or changing your mind. I didn't come all the way out to a cemetery to meet a Yankee girl for nothing. Tell me what's up."

Shana looked at the ground for a minute and thought hard. Her eyes focused on the promise ring that she was wearing on her right hand. "Ok," she said, "you'll have to follow me to the mausoleum though."

Dale and Shana walked up the hill and stopped just in front of the old mausoleum. "You may think I'm just a crazy Yankee girl when I tell you this, but I swear, it is true. The other day, I ran into this place for shelter from that big storm. When it was over, I heard a voice coming from just outside. I couldn't see anyone, anywhere, but I knew I wasn't alone. The voice seemed to follow me through the woods and I saw a girl. She was in the trees but disappeared when I got there. Do you know any girls that live around here? I thought you Darby's were the only other people around Pulltight."

"What did this girl look like?" Dale asked. "How old was she?"

"I don't know, I could just make out a figure. She looked like she had black or brown hair and may have been around 20 years old. I couldn't tell much more, because of the bushes. I think she's the one who dropped this ring. I need to get it back to her."

"Well, you're right, us Darby's are the only other ones living around here. It may have been some girl from Daggett. She could have been out to the creek with some other people, just messing around. Sometimes they like to fish or float out there."

"No, there was no one else around. It gave me this really eerie feeling. I can't really describe it. It just didn't feel normal. She kept repeating a word, over and over. It was like a whisper."

"What was she saying?" Dale asked, with an interested look.

"Triska. She kept saying the word Triska."

"Triska," Dale asked, scratching his head. "That sounds like some sort of foreign language. I wonder what it means?"

"I don't know but I'm curious to find out. Dale, do you think she may come back to this cemetery or to the creek?"

Dale plopped himself down on the steps of the red- bricked mausoleum and studied the area. "If I lost a ring like that, I would probably come back looking for it. I think I have an idea. You said you saw her here and in the woods, right? Why don't we leave a message for her. Let's get a couple of sticks and write that word you said in the dirt, in both of those places, and see if she replies. We'll come back tomorrow and if she does, we can leave the ring there, hide and see who she is."

"That's a dumb idea," Shana said, looking at Dale with disappointment.

"Do you have one that works better?"

"No, you have a point. I guess it wouldn't hurt to try it. Grab a stick."

Dale grabbed a broken branch and twisted off a good sturdy stick. In the black dirt, next to the mausoleum, he wrote "TRISKA" in large letters. Stepping back, he admired his work as if he had just written a great novel. "Brilliant," he said, bringing a chuckle from Shana.

"If you say so," she replied. "Now, I guess we can go to where I found the ring and do the same. I really think it's a waste of time though."

"Anywhere else is fine with me. I'm ready to get far away from this cemetery. Do you know why they put this big iron fence up around it?"

"Why is that?" Shana asked.

"To keep all the people out. Didn't you know people are just dying to get into this place?"

"You are morbid, Dale Darby. That's not even funny. I think your momma whipped you too hard with that race track."

Dale laughed and followed Shana off into the woods. He wasn't quite sure why he was going along with her but he had a feeling that something unusual was about to happen.

Chapter 5
Trista Marlin

"Dale! Dale!" Shana shouted towards the old cypress house. "Dale Darby!"

Soon, six faces appeared, looking out of the front door. "Dale's around back," a dirty faced little Darby said. "He's picking peas with Momma."

"Oh. Thanks," Shana said, turning quickly and making her way to the back of the house.

When she reached the back yard, she spotted Dale, wooden basket in hand, snapping peas off the vines.

"Dale Darby, did you mess with those messages we left yesterday? I want you to tell me the truth, too. No lying."

"I haven't been near the woods, cemetery or creek since yesterday," he said, wiping the sweat off his face with his arm.

"I can attest to that," Dale's mom said from two pea rows over. "He's been working in the garden with me all day today."

Shana studied the tired looking eyes of Mrs. Darby. Crows feet hung heavy on her face and dark circles formed under her eyes. It was apparent that she was once a redhead but now streaks of white were starting to form and take over. Her hands looked like leather and the dirt was thick under her fingernails. "You poor worn out woman," Shana thought to herself. "What a hard life you must have."

"Something wrong, girl?" Mrs. Darby asked.

"Oh, no Ma'am, Mrs. Darby. I just had something I wanted to talk to Dale about."

“Well, talk away,” Mrs. Darby replied. “Dale can work while he talks. He’s a multi-tasker.”

Mrs. Darby went back to picking peas and Shana walked along side of Dale, who didn’t dare stop working.

“Dale, if you didn’t mess with that message, then someone else did. It was all messed up and there were no footprints anywhere besides ours from yesterday,” Shana said, trying to keep her conversation away from Mrs. Darby’s ears.

“What was messed up?” Dale asked.

“The K. The K was wiped clean. It was gone from both messages. You could tell someone did it with their hand, too. There were imprints of fingers.”

“Who would just erase a K? It has to be some sort of message or code. What the heck does Triska mean anyway?”

“Triska?” Mrs. Darby asked. “Why did you say that? Have y’all been talking to somebody?”

Dale and Shana looked at Mrs. Darby with surprise. “Do you know what Triska means, Momma?”

“I don’t know what it means, but I know who it was,” Mrs. Darby said, sitting down her basket of peas with a look of surprise.

“Mrs. Darby, would you please tell us who?” Shana asked. “It’s been a mystery to us and it may help us return something that someone has lost. Please tell us.”

Mrs. Darby placed her hands on her sturdy hips with an expression that almost looked like a smile. It was as if she were looking through both of them, trying to recall something. “There was a family here in Pulltight around 30 years ago, last name of Marlin. They settled here from Oklahoma. I believe their car broke down and they just decided to stay on around here and do farm work. Not that I have room to talk, but they were a homely bunch, real plain looking. There was about five or six of them and every one of them had this same bad speech impediment. It was all a person could do to understand one of them. They were friendly enough, but you never could tell what they were saying. A lot of people made fun of them because of that strange impediment. I never could stand seeing anyone tease them. It's just cruel for folks to act that way."

"Cruel?" Shana thought. "This coming from a woman who whips her kids with a racecar track."

"The family had one daughter that was prettier than any of the other kids," Mrs. Darby said. "I remember wishing many a day that I was as pretty as she was. She had that same speech impediment, though. But she was just as sweet of a girl that you'd ever meet. She tried not to talk much. You could tell she was ashamed. Bless her heart."

"Was her name Triska, Momma?" Dale asked.

"Trista," Mrs. Darby replied. "Trista. But when she said her name, she said 'Triska' because of that dang impediment. So, that's what everybody called her."

"Oh, that makes sense why the K's were taken out of the name in our messages," Shana said. "Do you think Trista is still around this area? Maybe she came back for a visit or something?"

"No child," Mrs. Darby replied. "She wouldn't be back. She's dead. Has been for some years now."

Dale and Shana looked at each other as the hair stood up on their arms.

"Dead?" Dale asked.

"Yes, dead. Something bad happened to that girl. Listen, your Grandpa Bill don't mind me telling you stories like this does he?" Mrs. Darby asked. " I don't want you getting scared and him getting mad at me."

"No ma'am, he won't mind. He tells me ghost stories all the time. I haven't gotten scared since I was a little girl."

"Okay, then," Mrs. Darby said, giving Shana a stern glare. "It's been about 30 years ago, but Trista met a guy in Daggett. They were meeting up all the time and I guess getting pretty serious about one another. Her daddy didn't mind because he wasn't too sure that any of his daughter's would marry, you know, with their impediments and all. The guy would come around Pulltight almost every day. He really loved her, you could tell. He was just a big ol' country feller and whipped the tar out of anyone who ever made fun of Trista. I was proud to see a couple of them guys get it, too. They'd been making her cry just about all her teenage years."

"What happened to her, Momma?" Dale asked.

"Well, if you'll hush, I'll tell you," Mrs. Darby replied. "During that time, there were a bunch of wild hogs living out in these woods. My daddy never would let us go out there because they were so mean. They had tusks like knives. Some of the local men had been trying to kill them off, but there were a lot of them. From what I was told, Trista had been cutting through the woods by the old bottle dump and didn't come back home that evening. Her boyfriend was waiting on her at home and when she didn't show up, he and her daddy went looking for her. Poor thing, they found her out by the creek in some bushes. She'd been gored by one of those wild beasts. Had two big puncture holes right in the side of her neck."

"Oh, my!" Shana said, placing her hands over her mouth. "That's just where I was at the other day, digging through the bottles. I didn't know there were wild hogs in the woods."

"Not anymore," Mrs. Darby replied. "Trista's boyfriend was really broken up over her death. He hunted those woods day and night until not a single hog was left. Not even so much as a piglet remained. He had a personal hatred toward them. They had taken away his true love."

"Is Trista buried in Fletcher's Cemetery?" Shana asked.

"She is," Mrs. Darby replied, looking mournful. "Just towards the back of the mausoleum. I was still just a girl, but when something like that happened in Pulltight, all the families joined together. I was at the funeral and I remember it just as plain. I felt so bad because she didn't even have a headstone. Her family couldn't afford one. They just put a piece of an old mill stone on top of the grave to mark it. It just don't seem right, her not having one. I've had a mind over the years to try and make her something more proper. I may just do that one day."

"Is her boyfriend still alive, Momma?" Dale asked.

"Oh yes, he owns the garage there in Daggett. Gene Patterson's his name. It took him a lot of years before he could move on from Trista's death, but he finally settled with a local girl there and had a few kids. He's a good guy. I haven't seen him in years. I'm still wondering why you two are wanting to know about Trista Marlin? You've got me curious."

"Well, we uh…" Shana stammered.

"We heard someone say something about her at the theatre the other afternoon," Dale interrupted. "We just wondered who she was."

"Well, now y'all know and now you can get back to picking peas," Mrs. Darby said, snapping a few more peas off the vine.

Shana studied Mrs. Darby as she walked along beside Dale. "She must have been a nice looking woman when she was younger," she thought to herself. "I guess at least her husband still thinks she is. They keep having kids."

As the sun beat down, the sound of snapping peas could be heard throughout the Darby's back yard, drowned out only by the heavy thoughts of why Trista was making herself known to Shana and Dale. They would have to know more.

Chapter 6
I'm Stuck!

Grandpa Bill and Shana walked in the front door of Dewberry's Grocery store. Although the store was small, there was a certain excitement about walking into the place. The screen door snapped shut as the giant rusty spring attached to it did its job. There were all sorts of good smells throughout and a certain coldness coming from the old concrete floor. Over at the meat counter was Lester Bratcher. Shana had seen him many times before when she went to Dewberry's. He always wore the same old overalls and flannel shirt and talked about five octaves higher than a normal person. When Lester told a story, he always had the same saying, "Now here's the kicker," he'd say. When a person heard that, you knew he was about to spin a yarn.

"Can I help y'all?" Verdine Hardner asked from behind the meat counter. She was smoking a cigarette and had not flicked the ashes off in some time. Her dark red lipstick stained the white filter and Shana wondered why she wore so much makeup if all she was going to do was cut meat all day.

"You got any of that Virginia ham?" Grandpa Bill asked.

"Sure do, Hun," Verdine replied. "How much you want of it?"

"Two pounds ought to do."

Verdine grabbed a ham from the meat case and placed it on the meat slicer. The ash on her cigarette went almost down to the filter now and Shana wondered when it was finally going to give way.

"Where's ol' Polly at?" Grandpa Bill asked. "She usually does all the meat slicing doesn't she?"

"Oh, you haven't heard?" Verdine replied. "We had to let her go last week. She kept getting the strep throat and she was working back here with that stuff. All kinds of people kept getting sick from it when they bought the meat. We just couldn't have that. How many pounds did you say you wanted again, Hun? Two?"

"You know what?" Grandpa Bill said. "I think I'm going to skip that ham this time. I somehow got me a hankering for some of that frozen sausage.

"Oh, ok then," Verdine said, placing the ham back in the case.

"Grandpa Bill," Shana asked, "would you mind if I did a little walking around town while you shop?"

"Nah, go on. I'll probably be in here a while anyway. You know how ol' Lester is when he gets to shooting the bull. You can't hardly get away from him."

Shana went through the squeaky screen door once more and made her way downtown. She always loved looking at the old buildings. Each one had a date and the person's last name at the top. They would be remembered forever or at least until the building was gone. Today, however, she had one place in mind. Not the movies or the five and dime this time, but today, she was interested in Patterson's Garage.

Just down at the end of the Front Street sidewalk, Shana peered across the railroad tracks and made out the faded old sign that now read "ATTERSON'S GARAGE." It seemed that years of weathering had worn away the "P" and it had faded into the past.

Crossing the tracks, Shana reached down and picked up a smashed penny. "Some little boy must have placed this here and forgot to come find it," she thought. She placed the penny on a flat white stone so he could find it easier if he were to return for it. Patterson's Garage was about a block away and she was anxious to meet Gene Patterson in person.

"Help me. Somebody out there help me," a small voice cried.

Shana walked up to an old brick building, just next to the garage. There was a small gap between the two buildings, and that was where the voice seemed to be coming from. "Who's in there?" She asked. "I can see you moving around in there. Who is it?"

"It's Dennis Darby," The small voice said.

"Dennis? Dales little brother?"

"Yes, ma'am. Can you help me? I'm stuck."

"What in the world are you doing in that crack?" Shana asked. "It's hardly big enough for a cat to fit into."

Shana heard the whimper of Dennis as he spoke with a shaky voice. "Well," he said, "sometimes them fellers over at the garage throw their empty soda bottles in between this here crack. I crawled in here to get me some of them so I could cash them in at Dewberry's and get me some penny candy. Well, I got me four of them and that's why I'm stuck. I can't fit me and them back out of the crack."

"Dennis Darby, you let go of them soda bottles and come on out of there!" Shana scolded. "Come on now!"

"No ma'am. If I do that, I can't get me no sucker, no bubble gum, no nothing."

"Dennis, I have an idea. You let go of the bottles, come out of there, and I'll show you a way we can get them out."

Shana heard the clink of bottles hitting the ground as a dirty faced little Darby came sliding out of the crack. Tears had been streaming down his cheeks and left a clean trail through the dirt. "How you gonna do that?" he asked.

Shana looked around, spotted an old broom handle and quickly picked it up. "Ok, now I need some gum," she said. "Do you have any?"

“No ma’am,” Dennis replied, “but I know where to get me some. I stepped in a wad of it back up the sidewalk. I’ll be right back.”

Dennis trotted down the sidewalk and raced back with a big glob of chewed, pink gum in his hand. Shana took the gum and placed it on the end of the broom handle. She stuck it in the crack and slowly pulled out one of the bottles. “There you are,” she said, “one bottle. Now you try it.”

Dennis took the broom handled and pulled the other three bottles out, one by one. He looked up and smiled at Shana in amazement.

“There,” Shana said, “now you won’t have to go climbing between buildings anymore.”

“Well, what if there’s a bottle way back in a crack and I can’t reach it with my stick?” Dennis asked.

“Then you get a longer stick,” a booming voice said from behind Shana. Startled, she and Dennis both jumped and slowly turned around.

Chapter 7
Are you Gene?

"I thought I heard voices out here," a large man said. Shana studied him in detail as he spoke. He was very tall with a broad chest. He wore a red flannel shirt with the sleeves rolled up and had black grease around every one of his fingernails. He smelled strong of motor oil and looked as if he hadn't shaven in a few days. The black hairs were heavy on his face.

"I thought I heard someone calling for help," He said.

"That was me," Dennis Darby replied. "I got stuck in between these buildings when I was getting me some soda bottles."

"Well, we can't have that can we?" The man asked. "I'm going to board that crack up and from now on, I'll have everybody leave their soda bottles out here on the steps for you. You come get them anytime you want."

"Really? You mean it?" Dennis asked. "You won't let no other kid have them, will you?"

"No sir," the man replied. "Those bottles will be all yours."

Dennis's face lit up and he smiled a big dirty smile at the man, revealing his shiny red gums, where his two front teeth used to sit.

"And who might you be?" The man asked looking at Shana. "Are you looking for soda bottles, too?"

"I'm Shana," she replied "and oh no, I'm much too old to be doing kid stuff like that. I'm looking for a man named Gene Patterson. I need to talk with him about something."

"Well, I just happen to know that guy," the man said. "He's a pretty good ol' boy. Can work on a car pretty good, too. Do you have a car that needs fixing?"

"Oh, no," Shana replied. "I need to talk to him about a ring I found."

"A ring?"

"Yes, I think it may have belonged to someone he knew."

Shana reached in her pocket and held out her hand, revealing the gold promise ring with the bright green stone.

"You mind if I see that?" The man asked, holding out his hand.

Shana placed the ring in his hand and he looked as if he had just seen a ghost. "I know this ring. I know it well. I drove into Black Rock many years ago and bought it at a jewelry store there. I'd never seen one like it before. It was special and rare. I bought it for a beautiful young lady named Trista."

"Are you Gene Patterson?" Shana asked.

"I am. Where did you get the ring?"

"I found it in the woods while I was bottle hunting."

Silence hung in the air as Gene studied the ring. "It's been so long ago," he said. "How did you know how to find me?"

"Triska led me to you," she said.

"Triska?" Gene asked, his expression turning to anger. "Triska?!"

Gene placed the ring back into Shana's hand and quickly walked back into his garage. Shana stood still. She knew she had just awakened something from the past. Slowly she made her way to the opening of the garage and could hear the clanking of wrenches as Gene worked underneath an old Ford truck.

“I know this is hard for you to believe. I can hardly believe it myself,” she said. “I honestly believe Trista is revealing herself to me from beyond the grave. I’m not sure why. I think she is trying to tell me something.”

The clanking of the wrenches stopped and Gene Patterson wheeled himself out from under the old Ford. “I have to tell you something?” he said, with a most serious expression. “I think she is, too. You see these huge bags under my eyes? Those are from two weeks of sleepless nights. Lately, when I dream, it’s like I can see her again. She keeps calling to me. Sometimes it’s like she’s standing just outside my window, calling my name, but when I wake up and look, no one is there. Maybe it’s just my imagination. I don’t know. Maybe I’m cracking up.”

“I don’t think you’re cracking up,” Shana replied. “I think I’ve seen her, too. I found the ring just where she was standing.”

“What are we going to do?” Gene asked.

“I’m not sure,” Shana replied. “I really wish I knew. Maybe Trista will tell us.”

Chapter 8
Percival Edelberth

As Shana rode back home in Grandpa Bill's old truck, images of Gene Patterson's face flashed before her. He looked tired and weary. His voice seemed so sincere, as if he were hoping her story about Trista were true.

"Grandpa?" Shana asked. "Have you ever known there to be anything unusual around these parts. I mean, like anything supernatural?"

"That's a very strange question," Grandpa Bill replied. "I don't suppose you're talking about all of this UFO stuff you kids read about in the comic books these days, are you?"

"No, Grandpa, I really don't know how to explain what I mean. Do you ever recall a time where something so strange happened around here that it was hard to believe?"

Grandpa Bill rubbed the gray stubble on his chin, giving off a scratchy scraping noise. "You know," he said, "there is one story I never told you. My grandpa told it to me when I was just a boy. I believed him up until I was grown and figured out that such things just don't exist."

"What is it Grandpa?" Shana asked with excitement. "I want to know!"

"Well, he told me about this family that used to live around these parts when he was just a teenager. They were some well to do folks that came over from one of those European countries. They had a big ol' house that sat back at the edge of Mulberry Creek. They went by the name of Edelberth. They had about five kids that went to school with my grandpa. He told me that there was one, however, that stayed at home. There was something wrong with him."

"Was he sick?" Shana asked, hanging on every word Grandpa Bill spoke.

“No, I don’t guess that he was. He had something else wrong with him. Grandpa said he only saw him a time or two and he had a real pale blue skin and black circles under his eyes. They called him Percival. Grandpa’s sister got hired on with the Edelberth’s to take care of him, and she had some stories to tell. She said that his poor momma was just plum exhausted because the boy never slept. He cried all the time and scratched, pinched and bit the other kids any time they came near him. Once she went into the kitchen and he was cutting his own arm with a kitchen knife and laughing this deranged laugh. She said his blood was just as black as could be. He had some real problems. He never could have gone to the school with the other kids because the teachers wouldn’t have known how to handle him.”

“Why haven’t you told me about this before, Grandpa?”

“Well, your Momma don’t like me telling you ghost stories and such. She always said they’d keep you up all night and she’d be the one to have to deal with you. I guess you’re old enough to hear about these kinds of things now without worrying her any.”

“What do you mean ghost stories? Is Percival a ghost?”

“I’m not saying that,” Grandpa Bill replied. “However, a body can’t be sure, according to my grandpa anyway. You see, according to him, when Percival was about 20 years old, news came around that he had died. I guess he had some kind of condition. That’s probably what made his skin look all blue. I guess a doctor these days would tell you it had to do with a heart defect or maybe even inbreeding. But anyways, he died and they were going to take him to the cemetery out there where you hunt your bottles. They loaded the casket with his body onto the back of an old mule cart and tried to cross Mulberry Creek with it. That wasn’t a good idea at all. A big thunderstorm had just come through that day and the creek was terribly flooded. The cart wheels stuck in the mud and one broke off. The casket slipped off the cart and was taken away by the swift current. There was nothing they could do but watch it sink into the muddy water as it drifted away. A terrible thing to happen to a family.”

"Oh Grandpa, that's awful! Did they ever find the casket?"

"They did," replied Grandpa Bill, trying to recall the words his grandfather had told him so many years ago. "They found it two weeks later when the waters went down. It was empty and my grandpa said he knew why."

Grandpa Bill grew deadly quiet as he debated whether or not to finish the story. He wished he had never started it, but had come too far not to tell Shana the whole tale.

"Well?" Shana asked. "What happened to Percival's body? You can't stop now. I'm dying to know, Grandpa."

"Now keep in mind, my grandpa was always telling ghost stories and things to scare us kids, so there's a 98% chance that he made all of this up, but he always told me that Percival was still in those woods along the creek. He said one evening, he was out hunting and he came to the edge of the cemetery. He thought he heard someone crying or moaning over by at thicket so he made his way over. There, squatted down, he saw Percival. He was still dressed in a faded, torn, Sunday suit, the same one that he was wearing the day he was to be buried. His skin was still blue and he had those black bags under his eyes. Grandpa moved in closer and called his name. Percival looked up at him and made a loud hissing noise. Grandpa said he became sick at his stomach as he noticed Percival eating a dead rabbit. He said his teeth had changed as well and looked like those of a wild animal."

"Was he dead?" Shana asked in a shaky voice.

"It would be hard to tell. Could have been he never was dead to begin with and maybe in some sort of a coma. That water may have brought him to. My grandpa seemed to think he was dead, though. He said Percival lunged at him, so he fired a shot into the air that scared him, sending him running back into the woods."

"Grandpa? Do you think Percival is still out there?"

Grandpa Bill gave a loud chuckle. “No, girl, I don’t recon he is. That was a long time ago. If he was still out there, he’d be a dusty old skeleton by now. I think my grandpa was just spinning a yarn to scare us kids. He got a kick out of that sort of thing.”

“Just a yarn,” Grandpa Bill said once more as he hit the gas on his old truck and headed towards home.

Shana settled back into the truck seat. She had a lot on her mind, and now, thanks to Grandpa Bill, even more.

Chapter 9
Vampurrs

Shana kicked potato sized rocks with the tip of her shoes as she walked down the old dirt road that led to the Darby house. She felt that she and Dale needed to meet and try to put all of these strange pieces together. When she reached the front of the property, she spotted Mrs. Darby hanging clothes on the line. There on the front porch was little Dennis Darby and he was crying as he washed clothes in an old metal wash tub.

“Why Dennis, what’s wrong with you?” Shana asked.

“I’ll tell you what’s wrong,” Mrs. Darby interrupted. “Dennis here decided he was grown this morning and told me he didn’t have to do any chores. Well, he got the wooden spoon on his hind end and gets to do all the other kid’s chores. That means Dale is free to leave if y’all were going off somewhere.”

“Oh, I see,” Shana said, gritting her teeth and squinting. “Where is Dale?”

“He’s around back. Tell him not to stay out past dark, though. I’m making wilted lettuce salad tonight for supper and he won’t get none if he’s late.”

“I will,” Shana said, making her way around the back of the house.

Dale Darby was standing right in the middle of a cow pen, holding a baby calf. “Hey there,” he said, spotting Shana.

“Dale, what are you doing with that calf?”

“Well, I read that if you pick a calf up every day, by the time he gets to be grown, you’ll be strong enough to lift him. Can you imagine that, me lifting a grown cow?”

"Sounds like a good way to get a hernia to me," Shana said, shaking her head. "Now set that calf down and come on. We need to get to Fletcher Cemetery and try to make sense of what's going on. Maybe Trista will have another message for us."

Dale sat the calf down and the two made their way around front.

"Just a minute," Shana said. "I want to ask your mom about something."

"Don't do that," Dale replied. "She'll talk forever, and besides, she already thinks you and her are becoming friends."

"She does? Well, good. Maybe we are."

Dale rolled his eyes and trailed along behind Shana towards the clothes line.

"Mrs. Darby?" Shana asked. "You know a lot about the history around here. Have you ever heard the story about Percival Edelberth?"

"Oh gosh yes, child," Mrs. Darby said with a chuckle. "My granddaddy used to scare us to death with that story when I was a kid. He'd have us crying our eyes out some nights, worrying us to death that old Percival was waiting just outside the window. He got a kick out of scaring us with stories like that. He said old Percival was a vampurr."

"What's a vampurr, Momma?" Dale asked.

"You know, a vampurr. One of them things that turns into a bat and bites folks on the neck."

"Oh, a vampire," Shana replied.

"Yeah, that's what I said," Mrs. Darby said, putting her hands on her hips.

“Was there any evidence that Percival really existed?” Shana asked.

“Oh, I believe he really existed, but I don’t believe he was no blood sucker. My granddaddy liked to add his own details to stories and such. He was a terrible liar. He was also a known arsonist, too, which was bad, because he had a wooden leg. He caught the dern thing on fire a time or two. I pray to the heavens that none of my kids inherited his ways. He loved playing with fire and lied like a dog.”

“Well,” Shana said, “I think your kids are doing just fine. You’re a good mother and doing a great job. Even with little Dennis over there.”

Shana watched as Mrs. Darby’s sun beaten, leathery face, lit up into a bright smile. At that moment, she actually looked very pretty and less like a worn-out mother and wife.

“Well, you kids have fun and watch out for vampurrs,” Mrs. Darby said, returning to her laundry.

“Let’s get out of here,” Dale whispered. “I told you she likes to talk too much.”

As the two walked down the road, kicking rocks, Shana could still hear Dennis Darby crying from the front porch. It wasn’t until they were a good mile down the road that the sound faded.

Chapter 10
Peace?

Fletcher Cemetery seemed extra gloomy, as Shana and Dale walked under the magnolia trees and crunched through the old leaves. The place could have certainly used a little upkeep, more than the once a summer mowing that it normally got from a local farmer.

The wind blew in several clouds that soon covered the sun. The darkness made the inscriptions on each tombstone stand out. Moss clung tightly to many of the older white stones, covering their dates of birth and death. Suddenly, the breaking of a cloud placed a sunbeam upon an old piece of millstone.

"I just got me a feeling," Dale said with a startle. "You know like when you see a snake and the hair stands up on your neck? I got me that kind of feeling."

"Dale, do you think that's Trista's grave?"

"Momma said her family put a piece of a millstone there because they were poor. I'll bet it is her grave."

As Shana looked closer, she noticed what looked to be a fresh scratch on the stone, almost as if someone had been clawing at it with their nails. It was very light, but she could just make the words out.

"What does it say?" Dale asked, looking closer.

"It says, 'You should.'"

"You should what?"

"Hold on Dale, I'm trying to make out the last word. It's really faint."

Suddenly Shana moved back from the stone and covered her mouth.

"What? What?!" Dale asked.

"Dale, it says 'You should die.'"

"I just got the heebie jeebies!" Dale said. "Let's get out of here. I don't want to be here anymore."

"I'm with you. I have a very uncomfortable feeling as well. I don't think it's good for us to be here today."

Shana and Dale turned to leave when a sound in the nearby bushes caught their attention. It seemed to be coming from just beyond a large evergreen tree at the edge of the cemetery.

"Do you think someone is watching us?" Shana asked.

"I don't know. The footsteps sound heavy. Not like a squirrel or anything."

Shana and Dale stood still as the steps grew closer. Suddenly, the shadowy figure of a grown man appeared in the open. Shana recognized him right away.

"Gene?" She called. "Is that you?"

"Yes," Gene Patterson replied, "It's me."

Shana studied Gene's face. Black circles hung heavy under his eyes and his skin had a pale look about it.

"Are you okay, Gene?"

"I'm hoping that I will be," he replied. "I haven't been able to sleep ever since we talked last. And, when I did sleep, I had the most awful dreams. It was as if Trista were calling to me, trying to tell me something. In one of the last dreams I had, there was a vision of a headstone. It had her name on it and the inscription 'True Love.' I have been working on making the stone day and night since the vision. I haven't even worked on a car in days."

"Is that why you are out here?" Dale asked.

"Yes, I have it in a wagon, just over in the trees there. I'm hoping that this will bring Trista and myself some sort of peace. Will you two help me place it on her grave? I could certainly use the help; my energy is completely gone."

"Sure," Shana replied. "We'd be glad to help. Maybe it will be good for all of us."

Gene Patterson made his way back into the woods and soon came back pulling a wagon with a stone that was beautifully carved. The inscription read 'Trista Marlin True Love.'

With a little digging and struggling, Dale and Shana pulled the piece of old millstone from the ground, moving it up against the base of a tree. With a few grunts and groans, all three managed the get the new stone out of the wagon and carefully set it in place.

"I think it looks beautiful," Shana said. "I know she would love this."

"I hope so," Gene replied. "I sure do thank you two for your help. I do have a strange request, though. Would you two mind leaving me alone here? I need to have a conversation with an old friend."

"Sure, Gene," Dale replied. "We understand."

Shana and Dale made their way back into the woods, looking back at Gene. He was kneeling just in front of the headstone and saying something aloud, just as if Trista had been sitting there in front of him.

As they disappeared back into the trees, a strange cold breeze blew over them, giving them both a chill.

“What was that?” Dale asked.

“I don’t know,” Shana replied, “but I will sure be glad when we’re back on that old dirt road. I’m getting the heebie jeebies now.”

The two picked up their pace and quickly headed towards Pulltight road.

Chapter 11
Did someone die?

That night, Shana lay in her bed, looking at the open window. A light breeze made its way through the screen, giving off the smell of the sweet country air. A large lunar moth landed on the screen and beat its wings upon it, stirring up a small dust with its wings.

Shana slowly drifted off into a deep sleep. It had been a long day and she was exhausted, especially from the long walk to Fletcher's Cemetery. As she entered the other side of awake, she saw a young girl standing in front of her, just beyond some trees. She studied her as she came closer. It was as if the girl were floating and not walking at all.

"Who are you?" Shana asked.

She was very pretty and had a look of happiness on her face. Reaching out her hand, she touched Shana's cheek.

"What is your name?" Shana asked.

The girl tried to speak but struggled. It was as if her tongue were stuck to the roof of her mouth.

"It's okay, you can tell me. What is your name?"

"Triska," she replied. "Triska."

"You are Trista? Why did you come to me?" Shana asked.

Trista reached out, took Shana by the hand and led her into the trees. She recognized the area right away; it was where she hunted old bottles. The two walked along the homemade pathway that led to the cemetery. Just as they were about to enter the cemetery ground, Shana fell to her knees. Something was there, she couldn't see it, but it was powerful and would not allow her to enter. She knew she was up against an evil presence and she began to cry from the great fear that overtook her. Suddenly, Trista pulled her up by the hand, running with her back into the woods. Shana knew she was helping her escape the evil.

"Thank you. Thank you," Trista said, struggling with her speech.

Suddenly, Shana awoke in her bed, still trembling with fear from the dream that seemed more than real to her. Tears was streaming from her eye and she looked around the room, making sure no shadows were moving on their own.

After hours of lying in bed, unable to move from fear, a sunbeam gleaming through the window gave her a sense of courage and she arose, making her way into the kitchen.

Grandpa Bill sat at the kitchen table, sipping his coffee and looking at the wall as if something were wrong.

"Grandpa, is everything okay?"

Grandpa Bill hesitated before he spoke, giving Shana an uneasy feeling. "No girl, everything is not okay. Not today."

"What is it? Did someone die?"

"Someone did. A local man there in Daggett, Gene Patterson. They found him dead last night. I didn't want to say anything to you so late. I didn't want you to be scared."

"How did he die?"

"His wife found him at Fletcher's Cemetery. He was stone cold dead, laying over a headstone. His body had been drained of most of his blood and was as white as a sheet. The weird thing was, nobody found a drop of blood anywhere."

Shana's blood ran cold as she heard the news. Reality took on a whole new meaning to her and she realized that evil was running loose in Pulltight.

Chapter 12
Killing comes to an end?

Shana walked down the dusty sidewalks of Daggett on her Saturday trip to town. Grandpa Bill was conducting his business at the local shops and the mysterious events still hung heavy in her mind as she looked across at Gene Patterson's old garage. The grass and poison ivy vines were now taking it over and the dust looked thick on the tops of the cars that would never be repaired.

The local constable had spoken with her three times now about Gene's death and there were certain details she was holding back. The newspaper said that his death had been the result of a wild pig attack. It was the only thing that made sense. They had not yet stumbled upon the fact that the tombstone he was found on belonged to his first true love.

Shana couldn't help but wonder if Trista were responsible for this. Could she have been what Mrs. Darby called a vampurr? She didn't know, but one thing was clear, Grandpa Bill had forbidden her to go back into the woods or anywhere near Fletcher's Cemetery until the wild pig was caught or shot. Mrs. Darby was even keeping her kids close to the house. What was to be Shana's last summer of relaxation and fun, had turned out to be a nightmare.

Shana spotted Grandpa Bill through the glass window of Jim's Café. He loved to stop in there for a barbeque and glass bottled soda when he was in town. She made her way inside, just as the waitress was taking his empty plate from him.

"Did you get enough to eat Bill?" The waitress asked.

"No ma'am. I didn't get full at all. I just got tired of eating."

This brought a chuckle from the waitress. "You are a character, you know that?" She said walking away.

Shana sat down at the table with Grandpa Bill. "You hungry, girl?" He asked.

"No, not much. I haven't had an appetite lately."

"Well, I hate to spoil it even more, but I ran into the constable Bert Harris this morning. He's still trying to piece together the clues you gave him and maybe find out where this wild pig is at. No luck so far."

Grandpa Bill wiped his mouth and took a big gulp from the glass soda bottle. "You know," he said, "people always wanted me to run for constable of Pulltight. I just never could bring myself to do it though."

"Why not, Grandpa?"

"Well, it's the name. I just don't want anybody calling me constable. It sounds like something a body would get from eating too much cheese."

This brought a laugh from Shana and made her feel better. It had been a while since she had even so much as smiled and Grandpa Bill always seemed to have a way of making the gloom disappear.

"You know, Grandpa, I think I will have me one of those barbeques."

"Now you're talking, "Grandpa Bill said. "Waitress! If you bring my granddaughter one of those fine Barbeques, I'll give you an extra tip."

"I'll bring her a barbeque," the waitress said with a smile, "but, you can keep your tips. The last tip I got from you was a Yankee dime and a hug around the neck."

"You know me too well," Grandpa Bill said with a mischievous grin. "Well, girl, you enjoy your food, I've got more business to do in town. I'll meet up at the truck with you about 4 o' clock."

Shana sat back and took in the smell of the BBQ as she watched Grandpa Bill go out the front door and strike up a conversation with a group of men across the street. Suddenly, the group of men moved out of the street as an old pickup truck, driven by Herman Sellers, came barreling down Main Street.

As the pickup came to a halt, Herman laid on the horn and the men gathered around. People in the stores and restaurant made their way to the windows to see what all the fuss was about. As Shana gazed towards the truck, she saw Herman jumping around the back of his pickup. Walking outside and making her way through the crowd, she spotted the biggest wild boar she had ever seen. He was lying in the back, bloody and lifeless. His giant white tusks were stained red and he looked as if he weighed a good 1,000 pounds.

"I'll tell you what," Herman said, proudly walking around his prized kill. "I didn't pick him off with that first shot and he came charging at me. That second bullet caught him right between the eyes. He dropped right there at my feet."

Constable Harris came walking up to the truck with a grin on his face. "Herman, you old son of a gun, where did you ever find that big feller?"

"Well, Bert," Herman replied. "I was over there on the other side of Fletcher's Cemetery and heard him a rooting around, grunting and what not. I tried to shoot him at a distance but he turned on me. Would have killed me, too, if I hadn't been quick on the draw. He's a killer alright. It was in his nature."

"No doubt," Constable Harris said, putting his hand on Herman's back, "this was what killed Gene Patterson. I'm sure of it. We owe you a world of thanks, Herman. You've made this County safe again."

All the men in the crowd surrounded Herman and patted him on the back. He smiled and shook their hands, straightening his hat from time to time to keep it from falling off his head.

Shana made her way back into the café, she had hoped that what Constable Harris said was true, but she had her doubts. Serious doubts.

Chapter 13
A question asked deserves an answer

As the next few days went by, Shana tried to convince herself that all that had recently happened was just a strange coincidence and that Herman Sellers had somehow put an end to the nightmare that plagued the area. If only thoughts of Trista Marlin didn't hang so heavy in her mind.

Shana waited on Dale Darby to meet her on the old gravel road outside of Grandpa Bill's house. They had made plans to walk into Daggett and try to get some answers. Dale had not been persuaded that a wild hog had been the cause of all the strange happenings in the area. He had heard from one of his sisters that the local library had a history room in the back of the building, with local history dating back to the early 1800s.

It was a long hot walk along the dirt roads that morning. Shana brought along two glass bottles of cola that were now sweating and dripping on the dirt below her. They weren't quite ice cold but they were wet and tasted good in the summer heat.

"There it is," Dale said, pointing to an old brick building surrounded by thick hedge bushes. "You ever been in there?"

"No," Shana replied. "I usually spend most of my time at the theatre when I'm in town. I didn't so much as know Daggett had a library."

As the two made their way inside, they began to look around the shelves for something that might provide a clue to the town's history. The smell of old books hung heavy in the air. It reminded Shana of her school back home and she smiled, knowing she would not be returning to the place again after the summer.

"Look at that lady over there," Dale whispered, pointing to the front desk. "She looks like one of those Pentecostal women.

Shana looked over at the little old woman who sat quietly, reading a book. She wore her long hair up in a bun and her blue jean dress came down just above her ankles. She carried herself with much grace as she licked her fingers and turned each page. She seemed almost mysterious in a way.

"Go and ask her about the history room," Shana said, giving Dale a nudge.

"I will, I will. Just give me a minute and let me work up to it."

The elegant little lady suddenly set her book down and turned her attention to Shana and Dale, who were obviously staring at her. With a smile, she stepped away from the desk and approached the two.

"It's so good to see two young people spending their summer day in the library. You don't know how good it does my heart to see that," she said, placing her hand on their shoulders. "I am the local librarian, Miss Bessie. What is it you two are looking for today? Can I be of any help?"

"Well," Dale stammered, "we are, well, we heard that you might have a history room here."

"Oh yes," Miss Bessie replied, "we do have an excellent collection of local and county archives. Not many people come in and request seeing them, but I have to tell you a secret, they are my favorite. I have read every piece of paper in that room. We have everything from Civil War battles to pioneer families in our collection. Are you looking for anything specific?"

"Well, there are a couple of families we are interested in," Shana replied. "The Marlins and the Edelberths."

Miss Bessie gave the two a look of shock as she silently studied their faces. "I know those families well," she replied. "If you two will come with me, I'll give you what you need to get started."

Miss Bessie led the two into a small back room that looked as if it were once a closet. A table sat in the middle of the room with two wooden chairs that appeared to be a part of history themselves. Dusty leather-bound books were piled from floor to ceiling on handmade wooden shelves, that bowed in the middle from the weight piled upon them. They looked as though they could break at any minute. Reaching into a corner, Miss Bessie took two smaller books and laid them on the table. They were so old the pages were crumbling and flaking onto the table's surface.

"You won't find anything about the Marlin family in here," Miss Bessie said with disappointment. "I'm sorry but nothing was ever written about them. Most people around here knew them pretty well, but I don't guess they ever did anything memorable to write about. Maybe that would be a good project for you two? As for the Edelberth's, you will find them in this book. I'll leave you two to your research. If I can be of any help, please feel free to call on me at the front desk."

Miss Bessie gave the two a smile and made her way back to the front.

Dale quickly opened the book and carefully lifted the pages. It was the first time Shana had ever seen a Darby be careful about doing anything. He scanned each one until he came upon something that caught his interest. "Here they are," he said. "It talks about them right here."

"What does it say?" Shana said, pushing her shoulder up next to his and looking at the book.

"Not much, there's only about two paragraphs on them here. It talks mainly about where they're from, their home over on Mulberry Creek and birth and death dates. It names the mother, father and the five children. The odd thing is, they all have a death date, except for Percival and by what we've been told, he was the first of the family to die. I wonder why it wasn't recorded?"

"That is odd," Shana replied.

“I can tell you why,” a quiet voice said, coming from the doorway, causing Shana and Dale to jump in their seats.

Chapter 14
He's not dead?

Miss Bessie stood in the doorway of the history room, with a solemn look on her face. There were years of knowledge within the many lines and gray hairs that shown about her, and Shana and Dale were ready to hear what she had to say.

"Why wasn't his death recorded?" Dale asked.

Miss Bessie gave the two a stern glare, looking into their eyes so deeply she could almost see into their souls. "Some things aren't in the history books," she replied. "Some things are handed down from generation to generation with the means of being kept secret. Some things are known by only a few people in this world. Why are you two so interested in Percival Edelberth?"

"It's a long story," Dale replied.

"I like long stories," Miss Bessie said, "especially if they're interesting."

"It has to do with Trista Marlin and Gene Patterson," Shana said, looking at the table.

"I had just the same suspicion!" Miss Bessie exclaimed. "I'm going to tell you young people something. Something I've known for years about Percival Edelberth and something I know you suspect, too. I can see it in your eyes."

"Will you please, Miss Bessie?" Shana replied. "We've got to know the truth. It's been driving us crazy."

Miss Bessie closed the door to the history room and walked over to a large stack of leather-bound books on the floor. Taking a seat atop them, she looked like a neat little canary roosting on its perch. Squinting her eyes, she gave a very sweet smile and began her story.

"I was told the truth about Percival from my mother many years ago, when I was just a girl. She told me often, but also, I was told to keep it quiet and never to tell, only to pass it along to my family someday. However, I have no family to speak of, I am the last of my family, but today, I will pass it along to you, with the same warning my mother gave to me - keep it to yourselves and only pass it along to your families someday. Do you promise?"

Shana and Dale nodded their heads yes and leaned in, focusing intently on Miss Bessie's story.

"Percival Edelberth's mother and father were close friends of my family and his mother told my mother the whole story of his sickness. He was a normal boy in the beginning, much like his siblings. His only problem was he liked to disobey his father's orders and would sneak out of the house at night to play in the neighborhood. While they were still in Europe, his father had warned him to stop playing at night in the local cemetery. He did not heed the warning and continued to play among the headstones until way past the point of worry. His parents searched for him and found him in the early morning hours, lying at the edge of the cemetery. He was almost completely drained of blood and had two small puncture wounds upon his neck. His mother nursed him back to health, but he was never the same after that, always very sickly, pale and given to hearing voices. He swore that a dark being hovering above the ground bit him, not an animal like some of the locals believed. Others believed differently, however, and asked his family to take him far from their village. That is why they moved to this area. Percival grew more deranged by the day. He was more than his family or anyone else could handle, much like a wild beast that had been possessed. If you want to know why his death date is not in the book, it is simple, he is not dead."

An eerie silence hung over the room as Shana and Dale studied the words in disbelief.

"He is not dead?" Dale asked.

"No child. Percival Edelberth lives. He is responsible for the death of Trista Marlin and Gene Patterson. You see, Percival Edelberth is a vampire."

Chapter 15
They WILL feed

Had Shana and Dale not experienced so many strange events during the summer, they would probably have dismissed Miss Bessie as a eccentric old lady who had been cooped up with a bunch of dusty books for too long. There was, however, a seriousness in her voice and a sternness in her eyes as she cut to the chase about Percival Edelberth.

Miss Bessie straightened her hair and looked around to make sure no one else was listening to what she was about to say. "You see, "she said, "I know where he dwells. Every vampire has a dwelling and every vampire must be loosened for a season. This summer is that season, children."

"Is Percival Edelberth in Pulltight?" Dale asked with a concerned look.

"That he is," Miss Bessie replied. "Mulberry Creek to be precise. He and those he has infected over the years."

"There are others?" Shana asked.

Miss Bessie shot Shana one of her stern glances and nodded her head. "A few," she replied. "They are forced to awaken as well and wander the earth until the season is over. The only one true way to put them all at rest is to put away their master, once and for all. Until then, they dwell in unholy misery. And believe me, children, they MUST feed and they WILL feed."

A chill shot up Shana's spine as Miss Bessie made her way over to a shelf and took down an old book of maps. As she plopped it down on the table, the heavy dust made Dale sneeze.

"I'm about to show you both a very special place, "Miss Bessie said, opening the book mid-way and tracing her finger across an old worm-eaten map. "Here it is."

Shana and Dale looked down as her finger stopped on a spot just along an old hand drawn place that read Mulberry Creek. Along the creek sat a wooded area that read Edelberth Pecan Grove and Estate. "Just among the grove is where the old Edelberth mansion sat," Miss Bessie said. "It was a grand old place. Large timbers, decorative gingerbread accents, tall windows and a lightning rod shaped like a beetle right up on top of the roof. I loved the old place, but it fell into ruin many years ago and I'm afraid there isn't much left. The pecan grove has long since grown over as well. I doubt it even produces anymore."

"It sounds like an amazing place," Shana said. "It's a shame no one lives there anymore."

"Oh, but they do!" Exclaimed Miss Bessie. Her eyes widened and looked ten times bigger through her thick glasses. "Many live there. A garden with a grand decorative Fiske fountain sits just behind the old home site, there is a cellar just yards away, a deep root cellar that was once used to store canned foods and keep things from spoiling. If you find that cellar, you will find them. I'm sure of it. I sense they are there."

"Them?" Dale asked, twisting his head in confusion.

"Percival Edelberth and the others," Miss Bessie replied. "That is where they sleep and the woods are where they play and hunt. It is a dangerous place to be. I hope you have not been wandering about the woods on your own, children."

Shana wanted to tell Miss Bessie the truth, but all she could do at this point was sit quietly and listen.

"Is there any hope of Percival Edelberth and the others going away and not harming anyone else?" Dale asked.

"They will go away when they have fed, but they will be back. They have returned four times during my life and they will return again during yours. Unless. Unless Percival is stopped."

"How do you stop a vampire, Miss Bessie?" Shana asked.

"That is another lesson in itself," Miss Bessie replied. "One I hope you never have to learn. My advice is to stay out of the woods, especially away from Mulberry Creek and if you hear a rapping on your window at night or the high-pitched screech of a long fingernail dragging across your window, do not open it. Beware!"

Chapter 16
How to kill a vampuur

Shana watched Mrs. Darby as she swept off her front porch. Her forehead always seemed to be wrinkled as though she were mad. Probably because she had just whipped one of her children for something. Although they were properly and often disciplined, they just didn't seem to care and continued on with their strong-willed plans.

"Mrs. Darby," Shana asked. "May I ask you a question? Do you know anything about an old pecan grove over by Mulberry Creek?"

"Oh gosh yes," she replied, coughing into her dirty hand. "We would pick pecans on the halves there back when I was a kid. We used to go out there every fall until that time the wild hogs got so bad. Daddy told us to stay away then. I suppose it's all grown up now. Probably not a wild hog in sight either. I'm sure the chiggers would eat you alive right now though. You're not thinking of going out there are you?"

"Well, I was just curious. I heard that an old house place sat back there and I thought I might find some older bottles for my collection. Maybe even dig out the old privy if I could find it."

Mrs. Darby thought for a second, scratching her straw-like hair. "It's not too hard to find. You just go over the narrow part of Mulberry Creek. That's where the old ford was and the buggies crossed. If you walk about a half a mile, you'll start seeing those pecan trees; there's hundreds of them. At the end of that is where the old mansion sat. If it were me, I'd wait until Fall and go. That way anything out there alive would be under rocks and such and not out in the open to step on."

"I'd like to go in the Fall, but I will be gone away to school by then. I may venture out there just to take a look though."

Mrs. Darby leaned over the edge of the porch to spit on the ground. It was the first time Shana had ever seen a woman spit. She didn't know whether to laugh or ignore, it was just so matter of fact.

"Well, shoot, if you're going out there, take a few of my kids with you. It won't hurt them to get snake bit. Heck, it might even kill the snake. That way you'll at least have some company and won't be alone in case something happens."

"I was thinking of asking Dale if he'd like to go out there with me."

Mrs. Darby wiped the remaining spit off her chin with her forearm. "That reminds me," she said. "I've been meaning to ask you something. You ain't got feeling for Dale, do you? I've noticed he's been taking a lot more baths lately. I've had to pump water at least three or four times in the last two weeks. He's wearing me out."

"Oh no ma'am," Shana quickly replied. "Dale and I are just friends. We have a lot of the same interests, that's all."

"Well, that's good. I know he's my boy and all, but a smart girl like you could do a lot better than Dale."

Shana stared at the ground. She could feel her face turning a bright shade of red and hoped that Mrs. Darby didn't noticed.

"I have another question," Shana said, quickly changing the subject. Remember when you told us about the vampire stories your grandfather used to tell you? Did he ever mention anything about how to kill one?"

"Child, you do ask a lot of questions don't you. I really should be doing my chores instead of all this gabbing, but I just can't help it. There's something about you that just gets me to talking."

"I like talking to you, too," Shana replied. "It seems we have a kindred spirit."

Mrs. Darby chuckled and rubbed her chin. "I remember Granddaddy saying something about a preacher praying over some sulfur water that came out of a spring and giving it to some folks to keep in their houses. They were supposed to throw it on a vampuur if he ever came inside. He said it would burn him and he would run off somewhere and not come back. He also told me that he heard about a feller that killed one with a wooden tent pole. Stuck it right in the vampuur's heart. Those stories sure do make me think about when I was a little girl. You've got me half way feeling like a child again."

As Mrs. Darby recalled her stories, Shana took mental notes of everything she said. Little did Mrs. Darby know, but she was preparing an arsenal within Shana's head, an arsenal to take out a vampire.

Chapter 17
Pastor Alma

"Grandpa Bill," Shana asked, "can we go to church today?"

Grandpa Bill took a hard sip from his coffee. "Church?" He asked. "Why if I walked in one of them, the roof would fall in on me."

Shana laughed at the thought of that happening. "I seriously doubt that would happen. Haven't you always told me that one day you wanted to start going to church?"

"Well, I need to get myself right before that happens. One day I'll change all my bad habits and then maybe I'll go."

"I don't think that's the way it's supposed to work. I think you're supposed to go to church and then change."

"I don't know about that, "Grandpa Bill said, shaking his head. "I'd feel just smack dab out of place walking in there a flat-out sinner. How about I take you to church and I'll wait on you at the café? I'll have you a burger and cold drink waiting when you get out. Is it a deal?

Grandpa Bill stuck his big hand out to shake on it. Shana smiled and shook her head at him and before long they were on their way down the old dirt road in his truck.

As they pulled along the end of the road, Shana spotted the old wooden church. . It was white washed with a green shingled roof. A large bell stood just outside the front door and looked as though it had been painted silver many times. Grandpa Bill let her out of the truck and pulled off, heading to the café. The church parking lot was empty and as she approached the front wooden doors, she realized they were locked.

"The church must be closed," She thought. "Maybe not enough

people in this small town were showing up on Sundays."

Suddenly, she heard a creak as the door began to open a little. There stood a round little man with gray hair and piercing blue eyes.

"I'm glad you came today, but you're a little late. I just let everyone go home. I couldn't preach anymore over the sounds of everyone's stomachs growling."

Shana chuckled at the man. She could tell right away he must be the preacher. He wore a brown suit, blue and red striped tie and gold cufflinks. Although his clothing appeared a little outdated, he seemed very friendly as he smiled a sincerely at her.

"You could come back tonight if you'd like. Services start at 5. We'd love to have you."

"I may do that," Shana replied. "I'm Shana Dodson."

"I'm Pastor B.C. Alma. It's a pleasure to meet you, Shana. What brings you to church today? Are you new to Daggett?"

"No sir, I've visiting my Grandpa in Pulltight for the summer. I'm here with sort of a strange request and I was thinking that I probably needed some advice from someone, well, holy."

"I've had a lot of requests in my years here as pastor. Surely there is nothing too strange or out of the ordinary. Let's hear what you have to say."

Shana looked at the ground for a moment and once even thought of running away, but soon she found the words she was looking for. "Pastor Alma, do you have any blessed water?"

Pastor Alma looked at Shana and smiled. "Now why on earth would you want something like that?"

"Well, I just need it, that's all."

"Young lady, I think I know why you have requested the water. It is not a strange request at all, to me anyway. Let me explain something to you. You do have the time, don't you? I'm not keeping you from anything pressing?"

"No, I have the time. Please tell me," Shana said, feeling as though she were about to get the answer she had been waiting on.

"In this Universe, there exists two very present forces - one being good and the other evil. Or light and darkness as some people would put it. Some people live fully in the light and some try to live somewhere in between, but let me tell you, there are some who live fully in the dark. They know very well who they are and what their wicked heart's desire. If you are seeking to stamp out evil, you cannot do that with more evil, only the light can do that. You keep this in mind as you set out on your quest; I think you are on the right path so far. As for the blessed water, I have none in this church, but if it would please you, I prayed just a short while ago beside the well behind the church. Feel free to take of that."

"I will, thank you," Shana said.

"I hope that I have been of some help to you, young lady, and if I can be of anymore, I will always be close by. It was nice to meet you," Pastor Alma said, patting Shana on the shoulder and walking back into the church.

Shana watched as the old wooden doors closed and slowly made her way around to the back of the church. There sat an old rock well with a bucket and rope attached. Dipping the bucket, she pulled up enough water to fill two cobalt blue bottles she had brought with her.

Looking back, the church seemed so vacant and empty, not like when she had first arrived. Even the sign out front seemed faded and she could barely make out the words. The windows were covered in dust and the paint looked cracked. Glancing down at the well, she noticed a small bronze plaque attached to one of the rocks. As she wiped off the dust she read:

“In Memory
Of
Pastor B.C. Alma
A good and faithful servant”

Chapter 18
A meeting

Shaken from the strange experience, Shana opened the door to the café. She could see Grandpa Bill sitting beside the track-side window, his usual spot. Just to the right, along the old bar stools, two kitchen workers were sweeping up broken bottles and plates.

"What happened Grandpa?" Shana asked, taking a seat.

"Oh, you know how old Frankie Stewart is about playing jokes on people? He was sitting there at the bar talking with Johnnie Sams and when Johnnie wasn't looking, he switched his coke bottle with a ketchup bottle. Ol' Johnnie threw that bottle back and took a big gulp of ketchup. You should have seen the surprised look on his eyes when he swallowed that down. Ha! Haaaa! Frankie went to laughing and that's when the fight broke out. There were fists and plates flying everywhere. The constable came and took them out of here about ten minutes before you got here."

"Well, I hate that I missed that," Shana said, looking down at her cheeseburger and fries.

"Eat up, girl. I told you I'd have some food waiting on you."

As Shana stared out the window, she spotted a familiar dirty face looking back at her. It was little Dennis Darby. He was looking inside and licking his lips. There was now a noticeable clean spot where he had licked off the dirt. Shana smiled at him and his little eyes lit up.

"Grandpa, I'm not hungry at all. Do you mind if I take this out to Dennis? He'd probably enjoy it more than I would right now."

"Go ahead," Grandpa Bill said, giving her a wink. "The poor little feller probably hasn't had a cheeseburger in a good while. Them Darby's live by whatever comes out of their garden most of the time."

Shana soon appeared outside and saw Dennis still looking through the window. "Dennis," she called, "come here a second. I have something for you."

"What do you got for me?" he asked.

"How would you like a nice juicy cheeseburger and some fries? It's all yours."

Dennis put his hands in his pockets and looked sadly at the ground.

"What's wrong?" Shana asked.

"Well, my momma told me we ain't supposed to take no charity from anybody. I sure would like one, but I know she'd give me a whipping if I took it."

Shana looked at Dennis's dirty little face and felt as though she wanted to cry, but she mustered up a smile instead. "Why, Dennis Darby, this isn't charity, I would never do that. I just felt bad because I missed your birthday this year. I just wanted to give you a birthday present, that's all. Your momma will let you have a birthday present, won't she?"

Dennis's eyes lit up and a smile formed on his tan little face. As he raised his head up, at least three dirt rings appeared around his neck. Shana wondered when was the last time he had taken an actual bath.

"Birthday presents are different," he said. "I guess I'll be taking me that cheeseburger."

Dennis quickly grabbed the burger and took several bites. Shana could tell he was in heaven as he ate. She smiled, knowing that she had made his day, but there were many unanswered questions still heavy on her mind.

"Dennis, if I were to ask you a favor, would you do it for me?"

“Sure,” he said, with his mouth full of burger. “I’ll do anything for you.”

“Well, when you get home tonight, would you ask Dale if he will meet me tomorrow, about 9 o‘clock, by the edge of Mulberry Creek? The narrow part of it. I’ll be waiting.”

“Yeah, I’ll tell him and thanks for my birthday present it sure if good,” Dennis said with a smile.

“I’m glad you like it, friend,” she said smiling at the dusty little fellow.

Shana looked through the window, she could see Grandpa Bill looking back at her. He gave her a big wink and smile. Although he would probably never say it, she could tell he was proud of her.

Chapter 19
The Scream

Shana stood by the edge of the nearly dried up creek, she wondered if Dennis Darby had mentioned anything to Dale at all about meeting her. It was well past 9 am and the clouds hung low and heavy. The sun had not begun to shine through and it appeared that maybe it would not be showing up at all. Suddenly, she was startled by the distant sound of someone singing off key in the woods.

"Yankee Doodle went to town, riding on a turtle. Flipped a quarter and he saw a lady in her girdle."

"Ugh, Dale Darby," Shana said, covering her ears, "if your momma heard you singing that, she'd switch you good."

"What momma don't know, won't hurt me," Dale said with a smile. "Now tell me why I'm meeting with an old Yankee girl this early in the morning?"

"I think you know," Shana said, looking at the ground. "It's probably better that we travel early in the morning."

"You know, I've been thinking," Dale said. "All this vampire nonsense is just that - nonsense. I mean, think about it, do you really believe what that crazy old librarian said the other day? She was just trying to get us to read more books, probably. That way she can keep her job. It was all made up. She's nuts."

Shana glared hard at Dale and squinted her eyes so that her forehead looked like a large W. Taking the tip of her shoe, she kicked hard at the ground, sending dust and pebbles all over Dale, making him feel as though he had just been blasted with a shotgun.

"You dumb ol' girl. Why'd you do that for?" Dale asked, dusting off his face and spitting out some dirt.

“All I’m going to say is that you really shouldn’t think too much, I’m sure it hurts that tiny brain of yours. Now come on!” Shana said, grabbing him by the wrist and crossing Mulberry Creek.

The woods were overgrown and layers of leaves covered the ground from years of building up. Poison Oak vines swirled around many of the trees and the two kept their eyes to the ground, watching for copper heads and cotton mouths. Although they could not see any of the spiders, snakes and insects, they knew very well they were there and well hidden.

“Look,” Dale said, pointing up ahead to a clearing. “I think I see those pecan trees Momma was talking about.

The grass appeared much greener ahead and large pecan limbs were scattered about from the many years of storms that had passed. As the two walked through the trees, they could hear the crunching of old and new pecans beneath their shoes, almost as if they signaled to someone that visitors were approaching.

“I can see the house from here,” Shana said.

“Whoa,” Dale replied as he studied the old structure. “That is amazing!”

Although weathered and grown over with vines, the home, gothic in style, was nothing short of a place built for royalty. Gingerbread traced the roof of the dark home and an iron fencing appeared around the top of one of the house’s large towers. A grand porch circled the entire structure and Shana envisioned the Edelberth family gathered all about it.

“The door is open, do you think we should go in?” Dale asked.

“I’m not particularly interested in doing that,” Shana replied. “I’m more interested in finding the root cellar that Ms. Bessie told us about. I just need to see it for myself.”

Dale and Shana made their way through the tall grass, stomping down a path so they might have an easier exit should the need arise.

It wasn't long before Shana spotted the old Fiske fountain. It was green in color from the years of being exposed to the elements. Large decorative dragons surrounded the fountain to give it an elegant Oriental appearance. It was still a truly magnificent piece.

"According to the crazy library lady, the root cellar should be just beyond the fountain," Dale said.

"Dale Darby, don't make me kick dirt in your face again. Your momma will have to pump you some extra bath water tonight. And by the way, why do you make her pump your water? You should be helping her out instead. She works too hard."

"Did Momma tell you that? She likes pumping the water, she don't mind. She's always doing stuff for us. I knew it was a mistake when you two started talking to each other."

"Well, just grow up, ok? Start helping out a little more around there."

Dale gave Shana a frown as he tromped through the overgrown garden and soon spotted what looked to be a door leading down into the ground. "Well, there it is," he said. "There's your root cellar. Can we go home now? I don't like this place and the sun is certainly not going to come out anytime soon."

"No. Just be quiet a minute."

Shana made her way over to the huge wooden door. Two of the weathered boards were missing and she glared down into total darkness. As she listened, not a sound could be heard coming from the cellar hole.

"I have a question, what were you planning on doing if you did see a vampire?" Dale asked.

"Well, I came prepared," Shana said, pulling out an old cobalt blue bottle filled with water. “This is blessed water I got from the church. Your momma said that if you threw that on a vampire, they’d run away.”

“Ain’t that funny,” Dale said, slapping Shana on the arm, causing her to drop the bottle through the missing boards and down into the dark cellar.

The bottle seemed to fall forever before finally dropping and crashing to the floor below. Hair stood on end and fear filled every fiber of the two as the shrill sound of an agonizing human scream came from the darkness of the cellar.

“Run to the house!” Dale shouted. “Run to the house!”

Chapter 20
I wasn't holding your hand

Dale and Shana hunkered under an old table in the home. Their hearts beat quickly and Shana began to cry.

"Shhh," Dale whispered. "Listen."

From out past the old fountain, the creaking of rusty hinges could be heard and then the sound of heavy wood, thumping onto the ground. The air seemed as heavy as the black clouds that loomed outside and the two froze as the back door of the house slammed shut, leaving them in total darkness. Shana gulped quietly as she took Dale's hand and squeezed it tightly. Dale began to shake with fear as he heard footsteps slowly making their way across the floor. It seemed to him now that Ms. Bessie had not been a nut after all. If only he had listened a little more closely to her, maybe he wouldn't have followed that stubborn Yankee girl to the Edelberth house.

As the footsteps grew closer, they stopped just in front of the old table, stirring up a dust that made the two want to cough. However, they held very still, Shana still gripping Dale's hand with all her strength.

Suddenly, there was a loud crash as a heavy curtain rod gave way and fell to the dust covered, wooden floor, letting light into the room. A loud whoosh of the backdoor opening, revealing even more light, then a crash of the cellar door out back.

Dale took this as an opportunity to make an escape. "Come on!" he said, grabbing Shana by the arm and running towards the front door. Within seconds, it seemed the two were making their way through the broken limbs of the old pecan orchard. As they stopped to catch their breath, Shana began to cough from the dust that still hung heavy in her lungs. Looking at Dale, with fear in her eyes, she began to cry and he placed his arm around her shoulder, walking her back through the woods and to the creek.

Not a word was spoken between the two as they traveled, looking over their shoulder every now and then to make sure they weren't being followed. It was clear to both of them that something supernatural had just taken place.

"I'm sorry I cried, Dale," Shana said, looking very ashamed.

"Ah, you're just a girl. Girls cry. My sisters do it all the time. I don't mind."

"Were you afraid? I sure was."

"I wouldn't let nothing happen to you," Dale said, mustering up some bravery. "I don't think we should ever go back there again, though. And who can we get to help? Nobody would believe us."

"I don't know. Maybe if we told your momma or my Grandpa Bill they might help?"

"I don't think so. You know they wouldn't believe us. The only one who would is Ms. Bessie and she's an old lady. What could she do?"

"I think we should go and see her again," Shana said. "She's our only hope it seems."

"It's still early in the day. Do you think she might still be at the library?"

Shana kicked the ground a bit, looking at the shiny river gravel that was spread about. "I think we should go and see," she said. "And Dale, I apologize for kicking dirt on you earlier. I wanted to thank you for watching out for me at the Edelberth home today. Especially when you held my hand under the table. I don't think I could have made it through if you hadn't held it so tightly."

A look of shock and seriousness came over Dale Darby's face as he glared deeply into Shana's eyes. "Listen to me Yankee girl, I wasn't holding your hand."

Chapter 21
A past visit

Shana and Dale slowly opened the front door of the library and glanced inside. Miss Bessie was arguing with a small, skinny man who was angrily banging her desk.

"That's a double standard!" the man said, slapping a book down on the desk. "I ain't trying to be ugly, but it's just not fair! I've been wanting to check that book out for two months now and you knew it!"

"And I told you, Demus White, I'll let you check it out when I'm finished reading it!" Miss Bessie shouted back, slapping her fist down on the desk and leaning forward to meet him eye to eye.

The two glared at each other, eyes squinted and mouth's formed into bitter frowns, for what seemed to be minutes.

"I should have known better than to come in here and argue with an old beehive hair, crank of a senile bat like you," Demus said, turning and marching angrily towards the front door.

"And, I would have stayed in bed today and never stepped foot outside if I knew I would have had the displeasure of running into a bald headed, sawed off leprechaun like you, Demus White!"

Demus jumped a bit as he grabbed the front door and noticed Shana and Dale. He was in too much of a huff for pleasantries though and continued on his way, slapping his hat down hard on his shiny head.

Miss Bessie suddenly noticed the two walk in. There was still a look of anger on her face and her fists were clenched hard. "I'm sorry, you two," she said, straightening her hair. "That Demus White has a way of getting under my skin in the worst way. Everybody's skin, I suppose. He and his wife, both, are the biggest bunch of trouble stirrers in the town. They're not happy unless somebody else is miserable. I don't think they can get a restful night's sleep without ruining someone's day."

"If his wife is anything like him, I hope I never meet her. He's an angry little man," Shana replied.

"Well, I guess it's not really his fault he's so angry. His wife, the miserable thing, weighs a good five hundred pounds to say the least. If I had to fight over the last chicken leg, the last biscuit or the last piece of cornbread, I'd probably be just as angry as him," Miss Bessie said, giving a stern nod.

This brought a laugh from Dale, which also made Miss Bessie laugh. She soon loosened her fists, straightened her dress and the stern look seemed to fade from her face. "Are you two here to do some more research?" she asked.

Shana looked at the floor and felt as though she might cry again as the feelings of what just happened at the Edelberth home flooded her mind. Dale also looked down with a look of guilt and worry.

"Look at me!" Miss Bessie demanded. "Both of you look me in the eye!"

The two slowly raised their heads to face her, revealing to her everything she had already suspected. "You two went to the Edelberth house, didn't you? Don't you know how dangerous that was?"

"We didn't believe you," Dale said. "I'm sorry. I wish we would have listened."

Suddenly, Shana could not hold back her emotions and began to cry. Miss Bessie slowly walked over to her and placed her arm around her, giving her a bit of a squeeze. "You feel really helpless right now don't you girl? That's how he wants you to feel. He feeds off the hopelessness."

"Who does?" Dale asked.

"Percival Edelberth," Miss Bessie replied. "He craves your fear. It makes him stronger and I'm sorry to say this, but it makes your blood taste even better."

Dale shook at the thought of a vampire draining him of blood and chills began to form on his arms, revealing large goose bumps.

"I don't blame you for going," Miss Bessie said, walking towards the door, flipping the closed sign and locking the door. "I went myself when I was younger. I had to find out for sure."

"You? You went to look for Percival Edelberth?" Shana asked.

"Oh yes, it was not long after Trista Marlin was found dead. I had a feeling that the stories that had been passed down to me, were more than just a myth. The pieces were fitting together too easily and I wasn't always an old lady, I happened to be quite a looker back in my time. I had a young man who followed me around like a puppy dog. His name was Jasper Clemmens and I talked him into going out to the Edelberth house with me one summer's day. The place had been vacant for many years then, but was still a magnificent site. We decided to explore the place a bit and went inside. Jasper and I lit a candle and looked around at all the antique furniture and such and soon I spotted an old shelf, way over in a corner by itself. Jasper and I made our way over to it and shined the candle to it. It was one of those old, heavy European carved shelves. The Edelberth's must have brought it over with them when they came to America. I slowly opened the dusty glass doors and saw an old photo, realizing right away who it was. The pale look, the black circles around the eyes, it could have only been Percival. It was as though I were looking at a demon himself. He was almost transparent."

"Were you afraid?" Shana asked.

"No, just curious, but that's when something strange happened to Jasper and I both. We were hit with an overwhelming smell of death. It was strong and took our breath, sort of like when a mouse dies in the wall and begins to stink, only this was much worse. Suddenly, I felt something lightly touch my arm, I thought it was a fly and slapped at it. Then I felt another and another, but there was nothing there. Jasper jumped as he felt the same sensations. We both ran out of the house slapping at files that just weren't there. Then, I heard a noise coming from just beyond that fountain in the back yard. It was a demented laugh that sent chills up our spines, followed by the slamming sound of the cellar door."

"Did you see Percival? Was he there?" Dale asked excitedly.

"No, we both ran through those woods as fast as we could," Miss Bessie replied. "I never turned back until we crossed the creek. There were many times after that day that I wished I had went back and done away with that ravenous beast, even if it meant my own life, but I guess I was just young and afraid."

Miss Bessie took a big gulp. Her face was beginning to get that familiar stern look again and there seemed to be a fire in her eyes. "I'm not afraid anymore. I'm going back."

"But, Miss Bessie, no," Shana said. "You can't."

"I'm going back child! It's time to end this."

Chapter 22
Redheaded Skunk

It couldn't have been a worse day to go into those dense, dark woods. Shana and Dale had debated for days with Miss Bessie, encouraging her not to go, however, she was determined and nothing could change her mind.

Standing at the edge of Mulberry Creek, she looked as though she were dressed as a British explorer. She seemed well equipped with most anything a person could think of. Looking at the two, Miss Bessie gave a stern warning, "Remember, under no circumstances are you to cross this creek! This is my job. Understood?"

Shana and Dale nodded in agreement, cringing as a cool summer wind whistled through the trees, giving off a howl.

Miss Bessie crossed the shallow creek and disappeared into the overgrown woods, her figure soon fading into the shadows. Shana was torn between wanting to go and help her and hiding like a scared child away from the evil that lurked just beyond the creek.

"Did you hear that?" Dale asked.

"I did hear something," she replied. "It sort of sounded like your mother."

"I think you're right. I'd better go and see what she yelling about."

As the two neared the other side of the woods, they could make out the distinct cry of Mrs. Darby. She was shouting in all directions, calling out the name of her youngest son, Dennis."

"Momma?" Dale asked. "What's wrong?"

"It's your brother, Dennis." She replied. "He got himself into some trouble this morning. His sister told me he called me a redheaded skunk. I asked him if he told her that I was one and he said 'No, I don't know how she found out you was one.' I tanned his little hide good and he ran off into the woods. I've been looking for him for nearly an hour. You ain't seen him, have you?"

"No Momma, I haven't, but don't you worry none. Shana and I will look around and we'll find him."

"Yes, we'll bring him home Mrs. Darby," Shana said. "You go on about your day. He'll be okay, you'll see."

"Well, I do need to get back and weed that garden," Mrs. Darby replied. "Maybe I was a little too hard on Dennis. I declare through, I just don't know what to do what that boy. He's been the most trouble of any of my young un's and I'm losing my wits with age."

Mrs. Darby turned and walked back towards home. It was apparent to Shana that she really loved little Dennis as the worry still hung deep on her face.

As Dale and Shana walked back towards the creek, they spotted a familiar sight - Dennis Darby. Little Dennis was clear across the creek and looking back at them with a tear stained dirty face.

"Dennis, you get over here!" Shana demanded.

"No ma'am, I ain't going to," Dennis said, shaking his head. "I ain't ever going back home. That red headed skunk of a momma I got has done beat the tar out of me for the last time. I'm gonna live in the woods and eat berries and make me a teepee to sleep in."

"Alright, that's enough," Dale said. "I'm going across the creek and grabbing him up."

Suddenly, little Dennis took off like a thunder bolt through the trees.

"Dennis! You get back here you little jack rabbit!" Dale shouted.

It was too late, he had already disappeared into the thick woods.

“Dale,” Shana asked. “I know Miss Bessie asked us to stay here and not cross the creek, but I couldn’t forgive myself if something were to happen to Dennis. We have to go after him.”

Dale hesitated for a second and gave Shana a look of agreement. “He’s my brother. Even if I have to give my own life, I have to bring him back to Momma safe. I promised her.”

Shana and Dale each took a deep breath and waded across the shallow water of the creek. The coolness of the water made them feel as though they were alive and hope was in the air. It would be a test of everything they both knew, but it was a task they would have to take on.

Chapter 23
A Season in Hell

Miss Bessie, setting forth with determination, crunched through the old pecans left on the ground from years ago. She wobbled a bit as she tried to keep her balance in her boots. Up ahead, she could see the old Edelberth mansion. In a strange kind of way, it awakened the passion she had inside for the history of the area and the people who once settled and prospered in the area, however, she wore a stern look. "This is the day I have come to do two things," she mumbled through her teeth. "To destroy Percival Edelberth once and for all and to die doing it if need be."

As she approached the mansion, a dark cloud covered the sun, casting shadows across the property, giving it an eerie look.

"You know I'm here, don't you?" She said aloud. "If not, you will know soon enough. I've come for you Percival Edelberth. Show yourself."

Suddenly, the deranged laughter of an unseen figure came from just behind the house. The wind blew very strongly and there was a sound of a door falling from its hinges. Miss Bessie sensed she were about to come face to face with pure evil.

She slowly made her way through a beaten-out path in the overgrown grass and around the side of the house. As she came to the back yard, she spotted the cellar and approached it cautiously. A stale and musty odor came from the depths of the dark and evil pit. The door lay on the ground as if had just been ripped from its hinges.

Reaching into her bag, Miss Bessie, pulled out an antique Crucifix, which she had taken from the history room of the library. It had once hung in one of the Sunday school classes of the old Catholic church that had been destroyed by a tornado years ago. She clutched it tightly in her right hand, holding it out in front of her as she neared the doorway of the cellar.

Looking deep within the darkness, she gasped as she heard a laugh and saw four sets of glowing eyes, as if they had been the eyes of rabid wolves, glaring at her through their cave.

"Who's down there?" She asked, reaching for a large flashlight and shining it into the darkness.

Four human figures scrambled to one corner of the cellar, like rats, trying to escape the bright beam of the light. Miss Bessie could see that they each wore an outfit that was worn and dirty. Probably once a fine garment, suited for a formal party, or perhaps even a funeral.

As the eyes, glared back at her, she could make out one twisted face of what appeared to be a young lady. She gave forth a demonic presence, glowing eyes, sharp teeth and an odor of death. Miss Bessie's stomach turned at the sight of her as her heart pumped with fear.

"Who are you?" Miss Bessie asked in a demanding voice.

As the others hissed and moaned with the sounds of pain, the young lady answered with an accent that was distinctively French. "My father called me Fleur," she said, "and so do the others."

"I am looking for the one you call Percival," Miss Bessie replied. "Where is he?!"

"The good man of the house is not here," Fleur answered.

"Where is he?! I demand to know. I have business with him!"

"He is away on business, Miss."

"What business?"

"He is walking to and fro through the forest, seeking whom he can find. You see, we have been but a season in Hell and it is time to return once again and feed before we are to return again."

A sense of courage suddenly entered the heart of Miss Bessie and she clutched the Crucifix tighter and held the bright beam of the light on her demonic rats, that scurried in the cellar's corner.

As she prepared to enter the cellar, another sound caught her attention. It sounded as if it were a child crying, just across the yard and in the pecan orchard. "Oh no!" Miss Bessie cried.

Suddenly a blast like a raging wind burst through the cellar door, knocking Miss Bessie to the ground. She gasped for breath as she hit the ground hard. Fear set into her soul as she realized what had just happened. All the breath had been knocked from her by a demonic visitor of Hell and now someone in the orchard was in danger. She struggled to regain herself and feared it might already be too late.

Crawling around the side of the house, Miss Bessie still clutched the Crucifix in her hand. She wheezed and gasped, trying to once again fill her lungs with air. Across the yard, she could see a young boy, still crying, taking some fallen tree branches and placing them in the form of a teepee. From up above, a shadow lurked over the tree tops, it circled the boy like a hawk waiting to devour its prey. The young boy continued stacking the branches unaware of the danger he was in.

Miss Bessie pulled herself up, sitting on the dusty ground. Opening up a small suitcase, she coughed and began to prepare for battle. She knew she may only have just enough time to save the youngster.

"Dennis! Dennis!" Came two shrill cries from the edge of the pecan orchard.

Little Dennis Darby stopped in his tracks as he saw Shana and Dale approaching him. Determined not to go back with them, he turned to run, but that is when he ran into what he though was a pecan tree. Looking up, he saw a figure of a being that would haunt his mind even into his old age.

The figure was a young man in an old torn suit. His hair was ratted and looked as if it were stiff like straw. A musty odor hung about him and dried blood appeared on the corners of his mouth. His skin was a pale blue and his eyes were as the eyes of a dead man. As Dennis stood in fear, the figure smiled at him, revealing overly long and sharp teeth. There were marks upon the figures arm as though he had been cutting himself, but no blood would come out from his veins. A truly evil being named Percival Edelberth, stood face to face with Dennis Darby, and the boy shook violently.

Shana and Dale stood still, unable to move, as the figure reached out his hand to Dennis. Almost in a trance, Dennis reached back. Swallowing his fear, Dale began to cry, because he knew at that point, he would have to give up his own life to save that of his brother.

Running toward Percival, he grabbed his brother and pushed him aside, knocking Dennis to the ground. Shana ran to little Dennis's side, grabbing him up and wrapping him in her arms. Dennis shook but didn't cry. He seemed to be in shock.

Percival's smile soon faded and his attention turned to Dale. He lunged at him with his dirty, broken fingernails, lifting him from the ground and as though he were preparing to fly away with his body to the tree tops.

Dale's life flashed before his eyes. He thought of how he had never really been anywhere in the world besides the local small country towns. How he would never have a family, and in his mind, he could see his name carved on a small headstone in the cemetery.

As he prepared to die, Dale's thoughts were interrupted by the sound of a loud bang. He watched the face of Percival, which was only inches away from his, turn from victory into sadness. He felt Percival's grip ease and his own feet were now planted on the ground. Where Percival Edelberth had stood only moments ago, now lay only a torn and musty old suit. It was as though he had just faded into the earth.

Standing in front of Dale was Miss Bessie. She was dirty, a bit bruised and wheezing. An old musket ball pistol was in her hand still smoking. Walking over to Percival's suit, she placed the Crucifix on top of it and smiled at Dale.

"Where is that girl that helped me to the orchard?" Miss Bessie asked.

"What girl?" Shana asked. "We didn't see any girl."

"It was a young girl. It was almost like I knew her from somewhere, but I couldn't place where," Miss Bessie replied. "Right after I pulled the trigger, I heard her say 'Thank you.' then she just disappeared from sight. She was standing right over there by the house."

Shana walked towards the house and as the clouds cleared the sunlight glinted on something in a dusty spot of the front yard. A dull yellow ring with a green stone, was on the ground. Shana recognized it immediately, especially since this was the second time she had found it and there in the dirt, as though it had been written with a finger was the name "TRISKA."

"It's a gift, for you. It must be," Dale said, looking at the ground.

"Yes," Miss Bessie said, "a thank you gift. Her nightmare is over now, along with a lot of others. There will be peace now in this area. Peace it hasn't known in some time."

Shana picked up the ring and put it on her finger. Hugging little Dennis, she asked him if he were ok. With a look of exhaustion and tears in his eyes, he said, "I want my Momma."

"Don't worry, Dennis," Shana said, "we're going to see her now. She's really worried about you. Everything is going to be okay now. I promise."

Dennis wiped the tears from his cheek, leaving a big dirty streak across his face. Taking Shana's hand, the group of adventurers disappeared into the woods, making their way back to Pulltight.

Chapter 24
Down a Dirt Road

At least once in their lives, a person feels the need to return to their past. Perhaps it is to remember the good times or maybe even to feel young once more. Although many people may be gone and structures may have fallen into the past, the memories are always there.

As Shana walked through Grandpa Bill's old house, she smiled as she spotted all the jars of dirt he had collected throughout his life. If she listened very closely, she could even hear his laugh as he told her he owned some of the richest land around. "Oh how I miss you Grandpa Bill," she whispered. "What I'd give to take a ride into town with you once more."

Walking down the old dirt road, Shana passed the Darby place. It had fallen down and the old garden was overgrown with weeds. The family had long moved away after Mr. Darby died. She heard that Mrs. Darby had even remarried and had a few more children. If she closed her eyes, she could even hear the children playing and poor Dennis Darby crying because he had just got a whipping from his momma.

As Shana looked out towards the woods, she remembered a brave and adventurous woman who had once lived in these parts and put an end to a terrible evil. She knew that in those woods sat an old mansion with a magnificent pecan orchard, but she had no desire to return to them.

In Shana's mind, there were now smiles and heartache, then smiles again as the thoughts flooded her memory. Throughout her college years, throughout her short marriage and divorce, throughout hard financial times, throughout many a doubtful night, struggling to find her place in the world, the memories of Pulltight and the people in it always gave her a happy feeling. She had to come back just once more, if only to know it still existed.

"Oh, Grandpa Bill," Shana said aloud. "If only you were still here, I know you could tell me just what to do in my life. I'm so lost. You always knew just what to say and do to make me feel better."

As Shana walked down the dirt road, she picked up a potato sized river rock and tossed it towards the creek that crossed under the road.

"I wish you'd watch out there!" Called a voice from the edge of the creek. "The last thing I need is a knot on my head. Especially one from an old Yankee girl."

Shana walked to the edge of the bridge looking down. There sat a man along the bank, tossing small stones into the creek. A big smile spread across his face as his eyes met with Shana's.

"What might you be doing on this old road?" Shana asked, eyes straining to make out the man's face.

"Most likely the same thing you are doing here. Isn't it strange?" the man said. "You and I both at this dusty ol' place, so many years down the road, just remembering and trying to feel alive again."

"This certainly seems like more than a coincidence," Shana said in a surprised voice.

You know, a man named Bill Dotson once told me that there are things inside of us that we think are dead, but they're not. They just need to be awakened. He was a good man. A very wise man."

"Yes he was, Dale Darby," Shana said, sitting on the ground beside him. "Yes, he was."

The End

Made in the USA
Middletown, DE
03 August 2022

70491073R00054